Weezer
changes the world

David McPhail

BEACH LANE BOOKS   *New York   London   Toronto   Sydney*

To Andrea,
who saw Weezer before I did

BEACH LANE BOOKS

An imprint of Simon & Schuster Children's Publishing Division

1230 Avenue of the Americas, New York, New York 10020

Copyright © 2009 by David McPhail

All rights reserved, including the right of reproduction in whole or in part in any form.

BEACH LANE BOOKS is a trademark of Simon & Schuster, Inc.

For information about special discounts for bulk purchases,

please contact Simon & Schuster Special Sales at 1-866-506-1949

or business@simonandschuster.com.

The Simon & Schuster Speakers Bureau can bring authors to your live event.

For more information or to book an event, contact the Simon & Schuster Speakers Bureau

at 1-866-248-3049 or visit our website at www.simonspeakers.com.

Book design by Lauren Rille

The text for this book is set in Adobe Jensen.

The illustrations for this book are rendered in fountain pen and brown ink

on Strathmore Bristol paper.

Manufactured in China

First Edition

10 9 8 7 6 5 4 3 2 1

Library of Congress Cataloging-in-Publication Data

McPhail, David, 1940–

Weezer changes the world / David McPhail.—1st ed.

p. cm.

Summary: After an ordinary puppyhood, Weezer develops extraordinary skills

that make him a major influence in the world.

ISBN: 978-1-4169-9000-0 (hc)

[1. Dogs—Fiction.] I. Title.

PZ7.M2427We 2009

[E]—dc22

2009005537

As a puppy, Weezer was perfectly normal.
He did all the usual things that puppies do.

He chewed Billy's toys.

He barked at the clock.

And every once in a while—not on purpose,

of course—he tinkled on the rug.

Then one day, something striking
happened that changed him.

Weezer began to develop new interests and skills.

He could count to ten—and higher.

He helped Billy with his homework.

And he explained the law of gravity to Billy's class
during show-and-tell.

But Weezer wasn't just good with numbers.

No, he had good taste, too.

Especially about which drapes went best with the new furniture.

As he got older, Weezer took on more demanding tasks.

He predicted weather patterns and helped avert natural disasters.

He figured out how to encourage the rich to give to the poor.

(The benefit concerts were a sensation!)

Weezer worked alongside scientists
and doctors to help them find
cures for diseases.

He came up with formulas for clean water and clean air.

And he sat down with world leaders
to show them the way to Peace on Earth.

Then one day, something striking happened that changed Weezer—

again.

When Weezer didn't come home,

Billy went looking for him.

Finally, he found Weezer lying still beside the road.

Billy carried Weezer home and laid him on his bed.

A team of doctors was called in.

As news of Weezer's condition spread, people from all over the world sent cards and letters urging him to get well.

They vowed to carry on Weezer's good works.
They would feed the hungry and care for the
sick. They would keep the air and water clean.

And mostly, they promised to stop fighting.

Then, just like that, Weezer opened his eyes.

He was going to be all right!

Bells rang, sirens wailed, and a cheer arose across the land.

HOORAY
for
WEEZER!

Over the next few weeks, Weezer got his strength back.

But there was something different about him.

He no longer seemed interested in math or science or interior decorating. He paid no attention to the weather or the TV news.

Now his top priorities were chasing a ball or fetching a newspaper or playing outside with his best friend, Billy.

His days of changing the world were over.

Weezer had become a plain old dog again—

an ordinary, fun-loving, much-loved dog.

But the people of the world?

Because of Weezer . . .

they were changed forever.

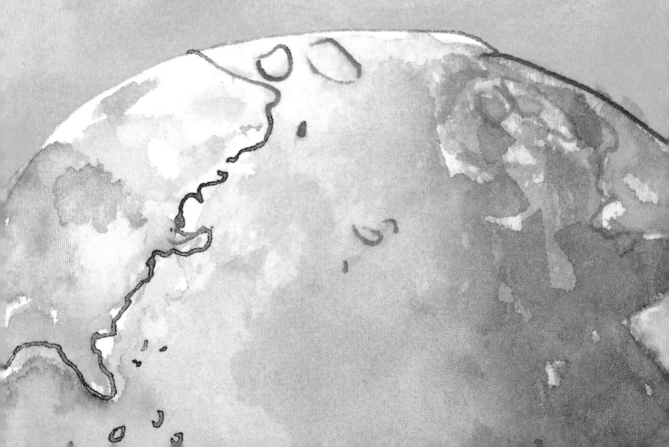